Mark Twain

A Connecticut Yankee in King Arthur's Court

誤闖亞瑟皇宮

Illustrated by Margherita Micheli

U0063731

The Commercial Press

Contents 目錄

故事錄音開始和結束的標記
start ▶ stop ■

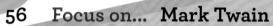

Characters

Hank Morgan

Clarence

Sandy

Merlin

Vocabulary

1 **Complete the crossword.**

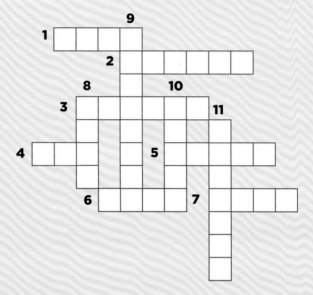

Across

1 a place where people grow food or keep animals
2 a metal suit for protection
3 a medieval figure who fights from a horse
4 it heats the earth
5 King Arthur's table is this
6 another word to say one time
7 the opposite of alive

Down

8 the chief noble in a country
9 a person who has supernatural powers like Merlin
10 an animal used for riding and transport
11 100

Grammar

2 **Choose the correct form of the verb in each sentence. Check as you read.**

When I (woke) / was waking up, I (thought) / was thinking it was all a dream.

1 Tomorrow at noon they *are going to burn / wanted to burn* you.

2 When she *spoke / was speaking* I *remembered / was remembering* the girl I loved in Connecticut.

3 Soon Merlin *decided / was deciding* to give in, so with my assistants I *repaired / was repairing* the well.

4 One day I *walked / was walking* in the valley when I *heard / was hearing* a voice in a cave.

5 They *had / were having* nothing and *starved / were starving*.

6 Sir Sagramor *was / is* in full armour but I *wore / was wearing* light clothes.

Listening

3 **Decide if you think the sentences are true (T) or false (F). Then listen and check your answers.**

	T	F
Hank Morgan starts his story with an accident.	☑	☐
1 He is hit on his legs.	☐	☐
2 When he wakes up he sees a man in armour on a horse.	☐	☐
3 He meets a young man who tells him he is at King Arthur's Court.	☐	☐
4 He meets King Arthur in person.	☐	☐
5 There are no women at court.	☐	☐
6 Merlin the magician is boring.	☐	☐
7 The people think Hank is a farmer.	☐	☐

Chapter 1

King Arthur's Court

▶2 I was at Warwick Castle in England when I met a stranger. He told me many stories about the past. I liked them very much. Then we saw some very old armour[1]. There was a bullet[2] hole in the armour.

"This hole is later. It comes after the invention of firearms[3]," said the guide.

"I did it," said the stranger, and smiled.

I was very surprised. The stranger was staying at my hotel. He came to my room and gave me a manuscript. His name was Hank Morgan. This is his story. ■

▶3 I was in my factory in Connecticut. A worker hit me on the head and I fell down. I woke up under a tree and saw a strange man in armour on a horse. He said I was his prisoner. His name was Sir Kay. I went with him to a village. He said it was Camelot. I was sure it was a lunatic asylum[4].

1. **armour:** 盔甲
2. **bullet:** 子彈
3. **firearms:** 武器
4. **lunatic asylum:** 精神病院

I thought all the people were mad. They all looked at my clothes. They thought I was strange.

I started to talk to a page[1]. His name was Clarence.

"Where am I?" I asked.

"King Arthur"s Court, in the year 513," he answered. "You are a prisoner. They are going to kill you. But I will come and visit you in prison."

Then some people took me to the King at his round table. There were lots of knights sitting round the table eating. Lots of people served them food. Beautiful ladies watched from a balcony. Musicians played on another balcony. The room was very big and made of stone. The knights' and ladies' clothes were beautiful.

An old man stood up and told a story. Everyone was bored and fell asleep. The old man was Merlin. Then Sir Kay told the story of my capture. He told a lot of lies and said I was very dangerous. He presented me to Queen Guenever. He said my clothes were magic. They took away my clothes and then put me in prison. I fell asleep. ■

1. **page:** 男侍

Mark Twain

4 When I woke up, I thought it was all a dream. Then I realized it was true: I was a prisoner at King Arthur's court. Clarence came to visit me.

"Help me to escape," I said to him.

"I can't," he answered. "There are lots of guards. And Merlin has put a spell[1] on this prison. No one can escape. Tomorrow at noon they are going to burn you."

I was very miserable but I had an idea.

"I am not afraid," I said. "I am a very powerful magician. Is today the 20th of June?"

"Yes, it is," said Clarence.

"Then go and tell the king that if he burns me, tomorrow the world will end in darkness. I'll end light and warmth. Everyone will die."

I knew from my studies that on 21st June 513 there was a total solar eclipse[2]. That was my magic: to make the sun disappear!

The next day they came to get me and tied me to a big tree. People sat to watch all around. Everyone wanted to see. I was afraid. And if my calculations were wrong? Then everyone looked up. The eclipse was beginning!

"Burn him," shouted Merlin.

1. **spell:** 咒語
2. **solar eclipse:** 日蝕

"Stop!" shouted King Arthur. "Have mercy! Do not destroy the sun. What do you want? I can give you anything!"

I said I wanted to be his minister and help him, and he agreed. The solar eclipse was now total, everything was dark. So I pointed to the sun and shouted, "Pass away and do not harm us!" The sun started to come out again and everyone was happy.

I became the first minister and the most powerful man in Camelot. Clarence was my assistant. I had beautiful but very uncomfortable clothes and the best rooms after the king. People came from all over the country to see me. I was famous, but they wanted another piece of powerful magic from me.

Merlin was in prison. He was my enemy, so I said I wanted to explode his tower with fire from the sky. His tower was an old Roman one and very solid. One stormy night I filled it with gunpowder[1] and attached a metal stick to it. Then I told everyone to gather, and we watched as the lightning hit the tower and it exploded. Everyone was afraid. They thought I was a very powerful magician.

1. gunpowder: 火藥

As time passed I realized that the people in Camelot were like children. They were very simple. They couldn't read or write and they were not logical. They believed everything they heard. I started to open secret schools and a secret military academy. I put down telephone wires[1] to have telephones. I wanted to create newspapers. I taught Clarence to be a journalist. The king and the nobles believed they were better than me because I was not noble, but they respected my intelligence. I thought I was better than them because I was intelligent, but I liked them. No one admitted all this and we got on very well[2].

After four years King Arthur was very happy with my work. He was richer because I managed his money well. I also distributed it better, and the people of Camelot were happier. They started to call me 'The Boss'. I liked it.

The main entertainment at Camelot was jousting[3]. Hundreds of knights took part and many were injured. Sometimes the knights went to save princesses from dragons. They believed in dragons and giants.

1. **wires:** 電話線
2. **got on very well:** 相處融洽
3. **jousting:** 騎馬比武

One day a girl came to Camelot. Her name was Alisande la Carteloise. She said her mistress and forty-four girls, many of whom were princesses, were captive in a castle. The guards were three huge men with four arms and one eye. At Camelot they decided I had to rescue them. I decided it was time for a holiday so I agreed.

I asked Alisande questions. She couldn't tell me anything.

"Where is the castle?"

"Many miles away," she answered.

"How many," I asked.

"I don"t know," she said. "They all look the same."

I got up early and had breakfast. Then I put on my armour. It took a very long time. There were many pieces and I couldn't move or do anything. They had to carry me out and lift me onto the horse. I felt like a ship going to sea. Then Alisande climbed onto the horse behind me. She had to show me the way to the castle. We started out and everyone waved good bye to us. ■

After-reading Activities

Reading

1 Say if the sentences are true (T) or false (F).

		T	F
	An American tells the story.	☑	☐
1	The man received an injury to his head.	☐	☐
2	He woke up in the sixteenth century.	☐	☐
3	There were a lot of people at King Arthur's Court.	☐	☐
4	King Arthur put the man in prison.	☐	☐
5	His friend Clarence was a knight.	☐	☐
6	The man said he was a scientist.	☐	☐
7	He survived thanks to a solar eclipse.	☐	☐
8	He became powerful and popular.	☐	☐

Vocabulary

2 Complete the sentences with the correct words.

A person you don't know is a...
A ☐ knight   **B** ☑ stranger   **C** ☐ minister

1 A text written by hand is a...
A ☐ manuscript   **B** ☐ book   **C** ☐ picture

2 Something which is strange is...
A ☐ difficult   **B** ☐ foreign   **C** ☐ unusual

3 Noon is another way of saying...
A ☐ midnight   **B** ☐ early evening   **C** ☐ midday

4 If something is in darkness there is no...
A ☐ light   **B** ☐ heat   **C** ☐ water

5 If something disappears you...
A ☐ can't hear it   **B** ☐ can't smell it   **C** ☐ can't see it

6 Something which is huge is...
A ☐ very small   **B** ☐ average size   **C** ☐ enormous

7 Two things which look the same are...
A ☐ a bit similar   **B** ☐ identical   **C** ☐ different

Grammar

3 Complete the sentences with a verb from the box in the correct form of the Simple Past, then check in Chapter One.

tell get go watch believe climb say take fall

He ....*told*......... me many stories about the past.

1 I .... with him to a village.
2 Beautiful ladies .... from a balcony.
3 He .... my clothes were magic.
4 I .... asleep.
5 They .... everything they heard.
6 No one admitted all this and we .... on very well.
7 Hundreds of knights .... part and many were injured.
8 Then Alisande .... onto the horse behind me.

Pre-reading Activity

Listening

4 Listen to track 6 and decide if the statements are true (T) or false (F).

	T	F
1 Hank meets a group of rich people.	☐	☐
2 The Freeman give Hank a present.	☐	☐
3 The Freeman are knights.	☐	☐
4 They have to pay tax.	☐	☐
5 The Freeman are repairing the bishop's house.	☐	☐
6 Clarence is teaching people to read and write.	☐	☐
7 Hank gives the men five pennies.	☐	☐

Chapter 2

Freemen!

▶5 We were immediately in the countryside. It was lovely and pleasant, very green, there were a lot of trees, fields and rivers. Then it started to get hot. Sweat¹ ran into my eyes. My armour got heavier and heavier.

Finally Alisande took off my helmet, filled it with water and poured it into my armour. I felt better. Alisande never stopped talking. I told her to take a rest and not use up all the air.

Night approached. It got dark fast. I found a place for Alisande to sleep and then one for me. It got very cold, and lots of insects climbed inside my armour. I couldn't sleep. In the morning I was cold, tired and hungry. Sandy was bright and fresh. ■

▶6 We set off. Suddenly we met a group of poor, ragged² people. I had breakfast with them and saw they were very happy. They were Freemen. They

1. sweat: 汗水
2. ragged: 衣衫襤褸的

were farmers and artisans[1], about seven tenths of the population. They were the only useful part of the population but they could do nothing without the permission of their lords or the church. They couldn't sell anything without paying tax[2]. They had to give part of their produce to the lords and bishops and work for them.

These men were free, but they were repairing the bishop's roads as part of their duty. I asked them: 'If you had a vote tomorrow, would you vote for a king?' They didn't understand, except for one man. He said, in a nation with a vote there are no kings or bishops. I decided to send him to my Man Factory, a school where Clarence was teaching people to read and write.

I gave the men three pennies for my breakfast. It was a lot of money but they deserved it. Then I lit[3] my pipe.

The next day we were crossing a meadow[4] when Sandy shouted, "Defend yourself! Danger!"

Six armed knights were in the shade of a tree. They attacked me. I lit my pipe. They suddenly

1. artisans: 工匠
2. tax: 税 ▶KET◀
3. lit: 點燃

4. meadow: 牧草地

stopped. Sandy said they thought I was a dragon. Then she told them to go to King Arthur's court and surrender, becoming my knights.

Sandy told me the story of the knights. It was very long. While she was speaking I remembered the girl I loved in Connecticut and I was sad. But then we saw a big castle.

Outside the castle I met one of my knights. He was my soap missionary. He went about selling soap because I wanted a cleaner country. He didn't manage to sell soap in that castle because someone died while they were using it. He told me the owner[1] was Morgan le Fay, King Arthur's sister. Her husband was King Uriens. Their kingdom was so small you could stand in the middle of it and throw a brick into the next kingdom.

Morgan le Fay had a terrible reputation, but at first she seemed very kind. She invited us to have dinner. Then a page touched her and she stabbed[2] him. She was very bad! Sandy told her I was 'The Boss' and she was very frightened of me.

1. **owner:** 主人
2. **stabbed:** 刺

I heard a terrible sound and asked to see where it came from. As I entered the cell I saw something I would never forget. A young giant of a man was stretched on a rack[1]. A poor young woman with a baby was in a corner. The man had killed a deer, a terrible crime. I told Morgan to free him and leave me with the family. The wife wanted the man to confess. Then Morgan would execute him quickly and stop his suffering. The man refused because the confession would give Morgan the right to take away all property from his wife and leave her with nothing. I thought: "This is a real man, a heart of gold".

I asked to see her prisoners. It was terrible. Some were there so long they had gone mad. A young bride[2] and her husband, separated by their lord on their wedding night, now didn't recognize each other. Morgan le Fay didn't even know who some of them were. An old man in his cell could see his home. He had a wife and five children. Over the years he had seen five funerals but he didn't know which member of his family was still alive.

1. **rack:** 拉肢刑具
2. **bride:** 新娘

I set all Morgan's prisoners free, except for one noble. I didn't care about him.

The next morning I was very happy to leave the castle. Sandy kept telling his stories. I met with my toothbrush missionary. He was very angry with my stove[1] polish missionary. Of course there were no stoves yet, but I wanted to prepare people for them and teach them about keeping a tidy home.

We had another chance meeting, with the old man who had watched the funerals from Morgan's prison. He was with his whole family now. The funerals had been false, a torture invented by Morgan. I was happy for him.

Suddenly Sandy said, "The castle! Look!"

"It isn't a castle, it's a pigsty[2]!" I said to Sandy.

"It wasn't enchanted[3] before," she said.

Sandy really believed she saw a castle with monster guards and captive princesses inside. So I paid the men who guarded the pigs to go away and rescued the "ladies". Sandy embraced[4] the pigs, believing they were princesses.

1. stove: 爐
2. pigsty: 豬舍
3. enchanted: 中了魔法的
4. embraced: 擁抱

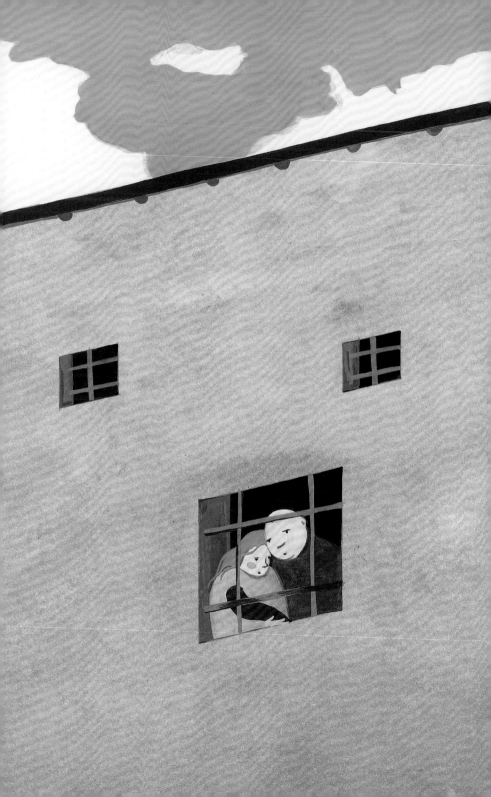

The next day we met some pilgrims[1] on the road. They were going to the Valley of Holiness, a place with a miraculous stream of water. Suddenly we saw a terrible sight. A group of slaves. Their clothes were dirty and torn. Their faces were grey. They were injured from the chains. A girl fell, and the guards hit her. Then her new owner arrived to take her baby and her away. She cried, and a man tried to embrace her, it was her husband. They were separated. They would never see each other again.

I still feel terrible when I think about that scene today. I will never forget it.

We arrived at a pub where I met a knight I knew. He was my "stove pipe" hat[2] missionary: he wore armour with a hat instead of a helmet. He said there was a terrible problem in the Valley of Holiness: the water had stopped! Merlin was there now, he was trying to make the water come back with magic. I sent a message to Clarence: *Send me pipes, extensions and two trained assistants.*

1. pilgrims: 朝聖者
2. stove pipe hat: 大禮帽

After-reading Activities

Reading

1 Complete the summary with words from the box.

bishop prison slaves pigs road pilgrims bad pigsty

Hank and Sandy continue their journey and meet some freemen. They are working for a ...*bishop*..... to repair a (1) .... Hank talks to them but only one understands the idea of a vote and no king. They arrive at Morgan Le Fay's castle. Hank realizes she is very (2) .... He asks to see her (3) .... and frees everyone. The next day they arrive at the castle Sandy told him about, but it is only a (4) .... The princesses are (5) .... Hank "frees" them and they continue. They meet a group of (6) .... and see the terrible treatment of some (7) .... Hank learns that there is a problem in the Valley of Holiness and sends a message to Clarence.

Grammar

2 Complete the summary with the past continuous form of one of the verbs from the box.

repair speak go teach try cross

They *were repairing* the bishop's roads as part of their duty.

1 Clarence .... people to read and write.

2 The next day we .... a meadow when Sandy shouted, "Defend yourself!"

3 While she .... I remembered the girl I loved in Connecticut.

4 They .... to the Valley of Holiness.

5 Merlin was there now, he .... to make the water come back with magic.

Vocabulary

3 **Put the adjectives into the table to say what they describe, then check in Chapter Two.**

tired lovely hungry cold heavy
frightened ragged pleasant poor bright sad
green fresh angry happy dark

Country	Armour	Night	People (positive)	People (negative)
				tired

Pre-reading Activity

Listening

4 **Complete the sentences with a word from the box, then listen and check. There is one extra word.**

happy coin military dress touched
nobles newspaper trip

Hank was not ..*happy*.... to hear about the king's new army.

1 Hank had a .... school and was training officers.

2 The nobles only wanted other .... as officers in the army.

3 Hank decided to go on a .... through the kingdom to see its general condition.

4 First he had to follow the ceremony where the king .... sick people to cure them.

5 The king gave the sick a metal .... for good luck.

6 Hank saw another of his innovations, a .... for people to read.

Chapter 3

The Holy Fountain

8 We travelled quickly with the pilgrims and arrived in the Valley of Holiness before sunset. All the people there were sad. I met the abbot[1].

"Hurry my son!" he said. "Save our valley or we will lose two hundred years of work. But do not use the devil's magic!"

"I only use God's work," I said. "But what about Merlin?"

"He promised too. But please, try immediately," answered the abbot.

"I can't," I said. "It is not fair. I must wait until Merlin stops."

I asked to see the well[2]. I made an inspection and realized that the well probably had a leak[3]. I went down the well and saw there was a big hole at the bottom. That was the problem, but I had to wait for Merlin to stop.

The next day I decided to visit some hermits[4].

1. **abbot:** 男修道院院長
2. **well:** 井
3. **leak:** 裂縫
4. **hermits:** 隱士

They were all very dirty and very strange. One had chains. One was naked and black with dirt. One stood on a pillar[1] and moved up and down. Eventually I attached a sewing machine[2] to him and made shirts. It made a lot of money.

Soon Merlin decided to give in, so with my assistants I repaired the well and put in a pump. Then we made a tunnel for the water to flow outside too. I put down some fireworks[3]. I called everyone and started the miracle. I said very big, strange, invented words. Everyone thought they were magic. Then I lit the fireworks, and the water started to flow. It was a huge miracle!

Soon after I asked if the monks wanted a bath. They were horrified: baths were forbidden because people having baths stopped the water in the past. But I told them it was a different problem that stopped the water, not the bath. They were very happy and loved the swimming pool I built for them to wash in.

One day I was walking in the valley when I heard a voice in a cave. It was one of my telephone operators! I asked to speak to Camelot and learned

1. pillar: 支柱
2. sewing machine: 縫紉機
3. fireworks: 煙花

that the King and the Court were coming to visit the Valley.

When I returned to the monastery I had a horrible surprise: a new giant magician! He said he knew what everyone was doing: the Emperor of the East, the Supreme Lord of Inde and others. Everyone believed him and was very surprised. I asked:

"What is my right hand doing?"

He didn't know! He was very worried. No one had ever asked that sort of simple question before. Then I asked, "What is the king doing?"

He answered, "He is sleeping in the palace."

Everyone was amazed, but I answered.

"He isn't! He is travelling by horse! He will be here in three days!"

No one believed me, but I checked every day with my telephone operators, and when the king was arriving I announced this to the abbot: people immediately stopped believing the false magician and believed me again.

It is not difficult to be a successful magician in King Arthur's time, but it is hard work and you can't rest!

9 When the King arrived he told me about his new army. I was not happy. I had a military school and I wanted to make my students officers. But when we had an examination of the candidates, the nobles did not accept my men. They only accepted other nobles, who were stupid and ignorant. My men were very well prepared but they were not noble.

Another problem with these people and their strange ideas!

I had another idea: a new regiment[1] consisting only of nobles, to keep them happy. And then the rest of the army made up of my soldiers, the real army. Everyone was happy.

I decided to go on a trip through the kingdom to see the general conditions. The King wanted to come too, and told me to wait. He had to do his ceremony. He touched the sick[2] and cured[3] them. Often it worked. People were convinced his touch was magic, and their belief made them better. The king did his best, he was a good man. The ceremony was very long and I was bored. He touched every sick person and gave them a coin. I decided to stop

1. regiment: 團
2. the sick: 生病的人 ▶KET◀
3. cured: 醫治

the gold coins and made copper[1] ones. This saved the kingdom a lot of money.

During the touching ceremony I saw another of my innovations, a newspaper! I was very happy with the result. It wasn't perfect, and I wanted to improve[2] it, but it was good enough and everyone was amazed by it. I was as proud of it as a mother of her new baby.

I suggested the king tell Queen Guenever of our departure but he was sad.

"When Sir Launcelot is here, the Queen doesn't notice if I arrive or depart," he said. I was sorry for him. I thought the Queen was beautiful but not very intelligent.

10 Later that evening I helped the king to dress himself as a peasant[3], ready for our journey into his kingdom. I cut his hair short: nobles had long hair cut short at the front, the peasants had short hair, and the slaves had long hair. I cut his hair like a peasant and gave him a long, simple tunic.

We left early in the morning. On the road, some noble people passed. I had to tell the king

1. **copper:** 銅
2. **to improve:** 改善 ▶KET◀
3. **peasant:** 農民

to bow[1] to them. He didn't know how to behave. He wasn't good at bowing and one of the nobles tried to hit him. I stepped in and he whipped me instead. Next, we met two knights. The king did not move off the road. He didn't understand that peasants had no rights, he believed the knights would ride round him. They didn't. They insulted the king who answered. This made them furious. To save the situation I insulted them more. They turned and started to attack us, so I threw some dynamite at them and they exploded!

The king thought it was magic. I told him I could not repeat it another time. He said:

"You must read my thoughts and stop me before I make mistakes."

"I can't," I answered. He was amazed.

"But Merlin can!" he said. I realized I had made a mistake. I said:

"Merlin can see a few minutes into the future. I can see centuries into the future. I don't bother with small prophecy like Merlin."

He was convinced.

---

1. to bow: 鞠躬

Vocabulary

1 Choose the correct end for each sentence.

The end of the day is at

A ☐ sunrise **B** ☐ midday **C** ☑ sunset

1 The problem with the well was:

A ☐ a hole **B** ☐ the water dried up **C** ☐ someone stole the water

2 The hermits were all very:

A ☐ clever and educated **B** ☐ well dressed **C** ☐ strange and dirty

3 When Hank first proposed the bath the monks were:

A ☐ delighted **B** ☐ appalled **C** ☐ confused

4 The unpleasant new arrival was a new:

A ☐ magician **B** ☐ soldier **C** ☐ noble

5 Hank wanted to train military:

A ☐ engineers **B** ☐ officers **C** ☐ doctors

6 The king didn't know how to behave as a:

A ☐ noble **B** ☐ teacher **C** ☐ peasant

Grammar

2 Complete the sentences with *to* only where necessary. Then check in Chapter Three.

I asked ......*to*..... see the well.

1 I decided .... visit some hermits.

2 Then I lit .... the fireworks.

3 The water started .... flow.

4 The king was coming .... visit the valley.

5 I announced this .... the abbot.

6 The king told .... me about his new army.

7 I wanted .... make my students officers.

Vocabulary

3 **Match the adjectives with their synonyms and their opposites.**

sad $\longrightarrow$ unhappy $\longrightarrow$ happy

1 strange	**A** not permitted	**a** interested
2 huge	**B** unpleasant	**b** ordinary
3 forbidden	**C** angry	**c** difficult
4 horrible	**D** unusual	**d** tiny
5 simple	**E** uninterested	**e** allowed
6 bored	**F** easy	**f** calm
7 furious	**G** enormous	**g** nice

Pre-reading Activity

Listening

12 **4** **Listen and complete the sentences with words from the box. Then listen and check. There are two extra words.**

> ~~couple~~ more ~~kind~~ noble mad less farmer nothing
> assistant food everything talked better rich

We asked for hospitality and the .....*couple*.... who lived there were .....*kind*......... .

1 I said the king was a .... and I was his ....

2 I paid for .... Everyone thought I was very ....

3 I told them that in my part of the country people earned .... but everything cost less. So in my part of the country people were .... off.

4 So I tried another subject. I .... about crime and punishment, and I said they were committing crimes by earning .... than was allowed by their lord.

5 The king started talking about farming. But he knew .... about it. The men started to say that he was ....

Chapter 4

The Yankee and the King

▶ 11 On the morning of the fourth day, when the sun was coming up, I decided to drill[1] the king.

"Sir," I said, "you are too like a soldier, a lord. This is not good. You must try to look poor and miserable."

The king tried to walk like a poor peasant but he was not convincing. He had too much spirit. I said to him: "What will you say when we ask for hospitality in a house?"

"Varlet[2], give me what you have!" answered the king.

"No, you cannot say "varlet", you are not a lord!" I answered. "You must say "brother"."

The king tried his best. "Give me the sack," he said. "I must try to stoop[3] under weights that are not honourable."

He tried, but it was very difficult for him to stoop. I thought about work. I thought about the people who believe that a day of intellectual work

1. **drill:** 操練
2. **varlet:** 僕人
3. **stoop:** 俯身

38

is hard. They don't understand that work is physical. It is silly to pay higher wages[1] to intellectuals than to people who work with their bodies.

We saw a very small, poor house in the distance. We arrived in the middle of the afternoon. There was no sign of life. Everything looked ruined and there was no living thing. We pushed the door open and saw some forms in the dark. One sat up.

"Have mercy!" cried a woman. "They have taken everything. There is nothing here."

"I do not want anything, poor woman," I said.

"Then you are not a priest or a lord?" she asked.

"No, I am a stranger," I replied. "Let me come in and help you. You are sick and in trouble," I said.

"Go away," she said. "We are in trouble with the lord and the church and we have the smallpox[2]. You must go away."

I told the king to go away, but he refused.

"The king does not know fear, and has no trouble with the church. I must stay and help, it is the duty of a knight," he said.

1. wages: 工資
2. smallpox: 天花

39

We gave the woman water.

"Please, go up that ladder[1] and tell me what you see," said the woman. The king went up the ladder which led to another part of the little hut. On his way he noticed a man.

"Is that your husband sleeping?" he asked.

"No, he died three hours ago. Now he is at peace," said the woman.

The king climbed the ladder and came back with a poor girl of fifteen. She was dying. He said there was another girl, who was already dead. He lay the girl next to the woman who sat with her until she died. I brought the other child to lie next to her.

The woman told us her story. They were persecuted by the lord and the church who made them work and took all their property. They had nothing to eat, and their three sons were unjustly in prison for a theft[2] they had not committed. Then they got smallpox.

At midnight they were all dead. ■

1. **ladder:** 梯子
2. **theft:** 偷窃

12 We continued our journey and came to a small house. We asked for hospitality and the couple who lived there was kind. I spoke to the man and discovered that he did not like the injustice of the country's laws. I liked him.

We stayed for some days with the man whose name was Marco, and his wife Phyllis. I said the king was a farmer and I was his assistant. One day I decided to have a special lunch at Marco's house. I invited a lot of people, all the craftsmen[1] of the town. Marco was terrified by the cost which was too much for him. I paid for everything. Everyone thought I was very rich.

At the lunch I tried to explain economics[2] to the men. I told them that in my part of the country people earned[3] less but everything cost less. So in my part of the country people were better off. They couldn't understand.

"But we earn double what you earn. This is better!" insisted one man.

"But we pay less than half of what you pay. Therefore we have more money and can buy

1. craftsmen: 手藝師
2. economics: 經濟學
3. earned: 賺取 ▶KET◀

42

more things," I replied.

They could not understand the idea which was new to them, and I could not explain it to them. I was very disappointed. So I tried another subject. I talked about crime[1] and punishment[2], and I said they were committing crimes by earning more than was allowed by their lord. This was a mistake. I thought we could laugh about it but they were terrified. They didn't know me and they were worried that I wanted to report them.

The king started talking about farming, but he knew nothing about it. The men started to say that he was mad.

"One wants to betray[3] us and the other is mad!" they shouted.

13 A fight started and the king was delighted, but I made him escape. We were in danger! We ran to the woods and hid in a tree, but the people found us and wanted to kill us.

Luckily a noble arrived and saved us. He took us with him to a nearby town where he had

1. crime: 罪
2. punishment: 懲罰
3. betray: 背叛

business. Then we had another terrible surprise. He took us to the market and sold us as slaves. He sold the king for seven dollars and me for nine. I was offended. I was worth at least fifteen and the king twelve.

We were chained to the slaves by the master who was hard and cruel. We got lost in the snow and five people died. Then a woman arrived screaming and tried to find protection with us. The people in her village said she was a witch and wanted to burn her. Our slave master helped them. We could not help her. Our master was angry about the dead slaves and revenged himself on this poor woman.

Then we saw a procession. A young girl of eighteen was sitting on a coffin[1] in a cart. She had a baby. With her was a priest who told her story.

She was a young wife and mother. Then the army took her husband away to be a soldier. She had no work and was starving with her baby. So she stole a small piece of linen[2]. The judge decided to hang her. The owner of the linen felt so bad he

1. **coffin:** 棺材
2. **linen:** 亞麻布

committed suicide. She cried and held her baby, but the priest, who was very kind to her, made a speech against the laws and the sentence, and promised to look after the baby.

There was gratitude[1] in her face when she died.

1. gratitude: 感激

Reading

1 Answer the questions about Chapter Four.

  1 Why was the king not convincing as a peasant?

  2 Why did the first hut seem negative at first sight?

  3 What three problems did the family have?

  4 Where were the woman's two daughters and three sons?

  5 What special occasion did Hank decide to organize at Marco's house?

  6 What two subjects did he talk about?

  7 How did the other men react?

  8 What happened at the market?

Grammar

2 Connect the sentences using the words in the box. You can use them more than once. Then check in Chapter Four.

> who   whose   where   which   ~~that~~

I must try to stoop under weights. They are not honourable.

I must try to stoop under weights that are not honourable.

  1 It is silly to pay higher wages to intellectuals than to people. The people work with their bodies.

  2 They were persecuted by the lord and the church. They made them work and took all their property.

  3 We stayed for some days with the man. His name was Marco.

  4 Marco was terrified by the cost. It was too much for him.

  5 They could not understand the idea. It was new to them.

Vocabulary

3 **Find the words for the medieval occupations and social positions in Chapter Four. The first letter is given.**

a military man: s _o_ _l_ _d_ _i_ _e_ _r_

1 a poor person who does agricultural work: p_ _ _ _ _ _ _

2 a noble man: l _ _ _ _

3 the highest noble, he rules the land: k _ _ _

4 a reasonably well off man who works the land: f _ _ _ _ _ _

5 a man who makes things by profession: c _ _ _ _ _ _ _ _

6 a person who helps another: a _ _ _ _ _ _ _ _

Writing

4 **Imagine you are the priest at the end of Chapter Four. Hank's friend Clarence asks you to write a short article about the experience for the newspaper. Write the article. Use at least 100 words.**

Before-reading Activity

Listening

▶ 14 **5** **Listen and say if the sentences are true (T) or false (F).**

	T	F
Hank managed to escape immediately.	☐	☑
1 Hank told the police he was a noble.	☐	☐
2 He sent a telegraph to Clarence asking for help.	☐	☐
3 Hank realized he could not escape.	☐	☐
4 He was very afraid when they started to hang the king.	☐	☐
5 Sir Launcelot and the knights arrived on horses.	☐	☐
6 Clarence was very happy about the result.	☐	☐
7 At Camelot Hank had to fight Sir Launcelot in a tournament.	☐	☐

Chapter 5

War!

14 I had a plan to escape. I had to wait for many weeks, but in London my chance finally came. Immediately things went wrong. I couldn't get the king's chains off! The slave master interrupted me. When he went outside I followed him and attacked him in the dark. But the police arrested me and put me in jail[1]. I said that I was a noble's servant. They were afraid of the nobles and let me go. Then I discovered that the other slaves had killed the slave master. They were all in prison, condemned to death[2]!

I found a telegraph station and sent a message to Clarence – *Send knights to save the King and I, they want to hang[3] us! Tomorrow!*

Everyone in London was looking for me. They took the slaves about London to recognize me. Unfortunately one of them saw me. They took me to the other slaves and decided to hang us that day. The knights would never arrive in time. It was too late.

1. **jail:** 監獄
2. **condemned to death:** 被判處死刑
3. **hang:** 絞死

They took us to the execution place. The King tried to say who he was, but everyone laughed at him. They started to hang the slaves. Then they started to put the rope round the king's neck. It was dreadful[1]. I couldn't move.

Suddenly a grand sight! Five hundred knights in armour – on bicycles! Sir Launcelot and the knights saved the king. Clarence was very happy.

"What a surprise, eh?" he said. "The boys practised for a long time!"

Soon I was home again in Camelot. I had to fight Sir Sagramor in a tournament[2]. Everyone came to see it. The knights all supported Sir Sagramor. Merlin did some magic to protect him. I only had Clarence to support me.

15 We started the fight. Sir Sagramor was in full armour but I was wearing light clothes. Everyone thought I was ridiculous, but I could move fast and avoid him. He couldn't catch me. He got very angry and wanted to kill me. I used my lasso[3]. They didn't know about cowboys and were amazed. I pulled Sir Sagramor off his horse and won the

1. **dreadful:** 可怕的
2. **tournament:** 騎士比武
3. **lasso:** 套索

fight. But Merlin stole my lasso and Sir Sagramor wanted to fight again.

I shot him with a gun.

Everyone was shocked. They thought it was magic. The knights were angry. Five hundred of them attacked me all at once. I shot some and the others escaped.

Everyone was afraid of me. For three years I improved the country. It was happy, civilised, with more money. Slavery was illegal. I wanted a republic but decided to wait until King Arthur died.

Then one day my child got sick! I was married to Sandy. I had married her because it was polite, but then I realized I loved her. I was totally happy with her. We had a daughter. Now she was sick. Sir Launcelot, a very kind man, helped Sandy and I to look after her. Then we decided to take her to the sea for her health[1] and sailed to France.

When there was no news I sailed back – everything was a disaster. Clarence explained that the king was dead, Guenever was a nun[2], the knights were fighting and the Church wanted to dominate the land. We had to fight! It was time

1. **health:** 健康 ▶KET◀
2. **nun:** 修女

for the revolution! We declared a republic, and the knights came to fight us. We hid in a cave and put dynamite everywhere. There were only fifty four of us, and twenty five thousand of them, but when they attacked we electrocuted them and then made them explode. We won!

Postscript by Clarence

I must finish the story. The Boss made a mistake. He went to offer help to some injured knights but one of them recognized him and stabbed him. Then we realized that our cook was Merlin in disguise. Merlin did some terrible magic and now The Boss is sleeping. He will never wake again.

Final Postscript by Mark Twain

At dawn I stopped reading. I went to the stranger's room and knocked on the door. There was no answer. He was delirious[1]. He spoke.

"Sandy, is that you? At last, now I can go back to you and our daughter! It was terrible without you! I am in the wrong century. A trumpet! It is the King!..."

He never finished his sentence.

---

1. **delirious:** 神志不清

Reading

1 Put the events from Chapter Five into the correct order.

A [7] Hank escapes from the group of slaves.

B ☐ He returns to England and tries to start a revolution.

C ☐ The police arrest Hank but then release him.

D ☐ Sir Launcelot and the knights come to save Hank and King Arthur.

E ☐ The other slaves kill the slave master.

F ☐ He leaves England with his family.

G ☐ Hank wins a tournament at Camelot.

H ☐ The police arrest Hank a second time and decide to hang all the slaves.

Grammar

2 Put the verbs into the correct tense and then check in Chapter Five.

I ..*couldn't*.. get the king's chains off! (can / not)

1 Everyone in London .... for me. (look)

2 We .... the fight. Sir Sagramor was in full armour but I .... light clothes. (start, wear)

3 They .... about cowboys. (not/ know)

4 I .... her because it was polite. (marry)

5 Clarence .... that the king was dead, Guenever was a nun, the knights .... and the Church wanted to dominate the land.   (explain, fight)

6 Then we .... that our cook .... Merlin in disguise.   (realize, be)

7 Merlin did some terrible magic and now the Boss .... He .... again. (sleep, never/ wake)

Vocabulary

3 **Complete the sentences with words from the box.
There are two extra words.**

> ~~afraid~~ wrong ridiculous grand full sick angry
> amazed polite dreadful

When he saw the dark shape, he was ...*afraid*..., absolutely terrified.

1 I was very surprised, really ....

2 That's very stupid, in fact it's ....

3 He's very ...., he always says please and thank you.

4 That is a .... idea, terrible!

5 Is the bottle .... or empty?

6 I'm sorry, but the answer is .... Try to give me the right answer.

7 She's ...., call the doctor!

Writing

4 **Imagine you are Clarence. Write an account of what happened after you had received Hank's telegraph. Use these words to help you:**

> ~~telegraph~~ knights bicycles practise leave
> ~~London~~ hang king rescue

Start like this:

One day I received a telegraph from Hank. He was in trouble in London! ....

....

....

....

....

....

Mark Twain

In the middle, Mark Twain - February 1871

Early Life

Mark Twain's real name was Samuel Langhorne Clemens. He was born in 1835 when Halley's Comet was near the earth. He grew up in Missouri, setting for *Tom Sawyer* and *The Adventures of Huckleberry Finn*.

His father died when he was 11 and he became a printer's apprentice. He spent his free time reading and studying by himself in libraries.

During a journey on a Mississippi steamboat, Twain decided to become a steamboat pilot.

He qualified in 1859. He also tried gold mining without success. In 1865 he published his first successful story. He decided that he wanted to be a journalist. He was a popular journalist and excellent public speaker. People enjoyed his stories and his travel articles.

In 1870 Twain married Olivia Langdon. He saw her in a photograph and fell in love. They moved to Connecticut, and had three daughters: Susy (1872–1896), Clara (1874–1962) and Jean (1880–1909).

His success

Twain was already a successful journalist when he published his first successful novel, *Tom Sawyer*, in 1876, based on his childhood. Its sequel, *The Adventures of Huckleberry Finn* (1885), is called "the Great American Novel". Twain was interested in science and in liberal progressive politics. He was against slavery and in favour of working people's rights. These interests are shown in his novels, *The Prince and the Pauper* (1881) and *A Connecticut Yankee in King Arthur's Court* (1889).

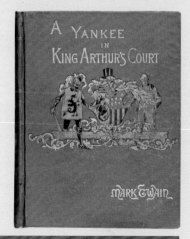

Later life

Twain was sad in later life after the deaths of Susy, Jean and his wife. In 1909 he said: *I came in with Halley's Comet in 1835. It is coming again next year, and I expect to go out with it. It will be the greatest disappointment of my life if I don't go out with Halley's Comet. The Almighty has said, no doubt: 'Now here are these two unaccountable freaks; they came in together, they must go out together.'* In fact he died in 1910 one day after the arrival of the comet.

Questions

1 Does anything about Mark Twain's biography surprise you?
2 Do you know any of his other novels? Have you seen the film versions?
3 Which one would you like to read?

Who was King Arthur?

King Arthur and Sir Launcelot, William Morris

Between reality and invention

No one knows if King Arthur really existed, but it is possible. Historians are not convinced, but say that perhaps he was a Romano-British leader of the late 5th or early 6th century, who fought against the Anglo Saxons to defend his country. Two early documents, from the 9th and 10th centuries, talk about him and say that he fought in the Battle of Mount Badon, killing 960 men by himself. He seems to originate from or near Wales. Many historians believe that it is possible only to say that King Arthur probably or possibly existed, but some say it is impossible and that he is just a literary invention.

Kings, Queens and Knights

Most of the characters we associate with him are certainly invented: Queen Guenever, Merlin the magician, Sir Launcelot, are all literary figures from Geoffrey of Monmouth's 12th century stories. He took some of these from other works, but he invented many himself. In medieval times, the stories of the King, Queen and the Knights of the Round Table were immensely popular. They were more about medieval society than real 6th century history. In the late 15th century Malory's *Le Morte d'Arthur* fixed the legends in people's imagination.

The legend lives on

After Malory, interest in the figure of King Arthur declined. But then in the 19th century poets and artists discovered him again. Wordsworth and Tennyson wrote about him, the pre-Raphaelite painters used the legends in their works. His popularity continued: Mark Twain used the legends, and Thomas Hardy. In the 20th century the First World War damaged the idea of chivalry, knights and noble battles. However, interest soon revived thanks to the cinema and popular novels. A stage musical, *Camelot*, also became a film, Walt Disney made the animated film *The Sword in the Stone*, even the comic team Monty Python made a film about King Arthur, *Monty Python and the Holy Grail*. One thing is sure: the legend lives on.

Questions

1 Why do you think King Arthur is so popular?
2 Are there any similar legends in your country? What do they talk about?

Test yourself 自測

1 Find and correct the ten mistakes in this summary.

Hank Morgan is an Englishman. He has an accident and wakes up in the court of King Arthur. There he saves himself from death thanks to a solar eclipse and makes a friend, Clarence. Clarence is a knight. Hank becomes the king's prime minister. People call him The Chief. Merlin is his friend. One day he goes on a journey with Sandy to save some ladies: the ladies are really horses. He meets the cruel Morgan le Fay and saves her prisoners. His second journey is with the King. They meet a poor woman who dies of influenza and then stay with a family. But there is an argument and they escape. A noble rescues them but sells them as farmers. The police almost shoot Hank and the King but Sir Launcelot saves them. Many years later Hank marries Morgan le Fay and tries to start a revolution. It fails. He returns to his original world and lives for a long time.

2 Complete the sentences with words from the book. The first letter is given.

1 Arthur is king of Britain and his wife is q.................. Guenever.
2 His knights meet at a r................. table.
3 Some people in the kingdom are the possessions of others, they are s..................
4 The powerful groups in the kingdom are the church and the n..................
5 Hank travels to the V................. of Holiness.
6 He tries to make the country better, to i.................. it.

3 What is your opinion of Hank Morgan? Who are your favourite characters? Why? Tell your partner.

Syllabus 語法重點和學習主題

//

Verb Tenses
Present Simple
Present Continuous
Past Simple
Past Continuous
Present Perfect
Past Perfect
To be going to
Conditional

Modal Verbs
Can, could, have to, will

Conjunctions
and , but, then, because, when

Relative Pronouns
which, who, where, when, that, whose

Lexical Areas
Medieval people, places and pastimes
Descriptive Adjectives
Town and country
Parts of the body
Clothing
Animals
Transport
Occupations

A Connecticut Yankee in King Arthur's Court

Pages 6-7

1 **Across**
1 farm **2** armour **3** knight **4** sun **5** round **6** once **7** dead
Down
8 king **9** magician **10** horse **11** hundred
2 **1** are going to burn **2** was speaking, remembered **3** decided, repaired **4** was walking, heard
5 had, were starving **6** was, was wearing
3 **1** F **2** T **3** T **4** T **5** F **6** T **7** F

Pages 16-17

1 **1** T **2** F **3** T **4** T **5** F **6** F **7** T **8** T
2 **1** A **2** C **3** C **4** A **5** C **6** C **7** B
3 **1** went **2** watched **3** said **4** fell **5** believed **6** got **7** took **8** climbed
4 **1** F **2** T **3** F **4** T **5** F **6** T **7** F

Pages 26-27

1 **1** road **2** bad **3** prison **4** pigsty **5** pigs **6** pilgrims **7** slaves
2 **1** was teaching **2** were crossing **3** was speaking **4** were going **5** was trying
3

Country	Armour	Night	People (positive)	People (negative)
lovely pleasant green	heavy	dark cold	bright fresh happy	tired hungry poor ragged sad frightened angry

4 **1** military **2** nobles **3** trip **4** touched **5** coin **6** newspaper

Pages 36-37

1 **1** A **2** C **3** B **4** A **5** B **6** C
2 The sentences with to are: 1, 3, 4, 5, 7
3 **1** D b **2** G d **3** A e **4** B g **5** F c **6** E a **7** C f
4 **1** farmer, assistant **2** everything, rich **3** less, better **4** talked, more **5** nothing, mad

Pages 46-47

(suggested answers)
1 **1** He had too much spirit.
2 There was no sign of life. Everything looked ruined and there was no living thing.
3 They had problems with the lord, the church and smallpox.
4 The two daughters were dead or dying in the hut, the three sons were in prison.
5 He decided to have a lunch.
6 He talked about economics and about crime and punishment.
7 They were terrified and attacked him.
8 He and the king were sold as slaves.
2 **1** It is silly to pay higher wages to intellectuals than to people who work with their bodies.
2 They were persecuted by the lord and the church who made them work and took all their property.
3 We stayed for some days with the man whose name was Marco.
4 Marco was terrified by the cost which was too much for him.
5 They could not understand the idea which was new to them.

3 **1** peasant **2** lord **3** king **4** farmer **5** craftsman **6** assistant

4 Sample Answer

I had to assist a young woman. She was eighteen years old. She was a wife and mother, but the lord took away her husband as a soldier. She had no money and was starving, so she stole a piece of linen to sell for food for her baby. She was arrested and the judge decided to hang her for theft. The owner of the linen was very sad and committed suicide. I assisted the woman before they hanged her. I spoke against the sentence and the law. Then I promised to take care of her baby. She was grateful.

5 **1** F **2** T **3** T **4** T **5** F **6** T **7** F

Pages 54-55

1 **1** A **2** E **3** C **4** H **5** D **6** G **7** F **8** B

2 **1** was looking **2** started, was wearing **3** didn't know **4** married **5** explained, were fighting **6** realised, was **7** is sleeping, will never wake

3 **1** amazed **2** ridiculous **3** polite **4** dreadful **5** full **6** wrong **7** sick

4 *One day I received a telegraph from Hank. He was in trouble in London*! I called the knights. The knights could ride bicycles because they practiced. They were very fast. Five hundred of them took the bicycles and they immediately left for London. They wanted to save the king. They were in time! The police were hanging the slaves. They hanged two slaves and now they were trying to hang the king. Hank was also at the erection place. He was terrified, he couldn't move or speak. But the knights surrounded the platform and stopped the execution. They rescued King Arthur and Hank. The people were all afraid and asked the king's pardon. They didn't recognise him because he was dirty and poor. Then they went home to Camelot.

Page 57

1, 2, 3 personal answers.

Page 59

1, 2 personal answers.

Page 60

1 **1** Englishman – American **2** knight – page **3** The Chief – The Boss **4** friend – enemy **5** horses – pigs **6** influenza – smallpox **7** farmers – slaves **8** shoot – hang **9** Morgan le Fay – Sandy **10** lives for a long time – dies

2 **1** queen **2** round **3** slaves **4** nobles **5** Valley **6** improve

3 personal answers.

Read for Pleasure: *A Connecticut Yankee in King Arthur's Court* 誤闖亞瑟皇宮

作　　者：	Mark Twain
改　　寫：	Jane Bowie
繪　　畫：	Margherita Micheli
照　　片：	Shutterstock
責任編輯：	黃家麗
封面設計：	涂　慧　丁　意
出　　版：	商務印書館（香港）有限公司
	香港筲箕灣耀興道 3 號東滙廣場 8 樓
	http://www.commercialpress.com.hk
發　　行：	香港聯合書刊物流有限公司
	香港新界大埔汀麗路 36 號中華商務印刷大廈 3 字樓
印　　刷：	中華商務彩色印刷有限公司
	香港新界大埔汀麗路 36 號中華商務印刷大廈 14 字樓
版　　次：	2017 年 7 月第 1 版第 1 次印刷
	© 2017 商務印書館（香港）有限公司
	ISBN 978 962 07 0461 1
	Printed in Hong Kong